When Christmas Comes

Written & illustrated by

Beverly Barron Gebauer

Dedicated With Love

To my husband, Edward

To my children - Laurie, Edward and Amy

To family and friends

And to my Heavenly Father

ISBN 0-9661082-0-5

Contents

LITTLE
SHEPHERD BOY

Dear little Shepherd boy, of long ago
Oh, How very blessed you were to know
Little Jesus, pure and small,
God's greatest gift of love to all
Who would come to know and serve Him, here below.

Radiant stars poured down their silver light
Glistening through the deep blue velvet night,
Angel voices filled the earth
To proclaim His Holy birth,
And leave your eyes, with wonder, shining bright.

Did you follow that bright star to where He lay,
Sweetly sleeping on that little mound of hay
Or, did you watch the whole night through,
Those little lambs who trusted you
To keep them safe until the coming day?

Where are you little Shepherd boy, tonight
When all the Christmas lights of home, burn bright
Are you watching from above
Every home that's filled with love,
Taught by One Who came to earth that Holy Night?

1

ONE SMALL HEART

The bells in the old Church steeple rang, and their glorious song echoed over the countryside. Old Elizer Mouse "scrumbled and bumbled" on his way along a dark passage over the rafters and up the rickety wooden steps to the bell tower. He moved along slowly, his tired little eyes squinting in the darkness. At the top of the stairway he waited patiently for the bells to be still. Then, climbing up the worn rope, he settled down on the top of one of the giant bells. From this lofty perch, he could see for miles. A deep carpet of newly fallen snow sparkled over the meadow. The river wound a silver ribbon through the woods.

"Oh! It's so be-ewe-ti-ful!" he whispered. "I can see the whole world!"

Now that was partly true, for Elizer COULD see all the borders of his own little world, everywhere he had ever scampered since he was a tiny church mouse. There were the deep woods, the river, the meadow. He could see Farmer Jacob's barn, the wide cornfield, and the kitchen garden behind the

2

farmhouse where he had gathered seeds and hidden from the farmer's cat. Now he was too old to venture far from the little country church. In life there were few pleasures left for him to enjoy. He longed for days gone by.

"Tonight," he promised himself, "I will not be sad. Tonight is different…special." It was Christmas Eve.

Every Christmas Eve, for as long as he could remember, he had climbed the long passage to the steeple. When the bells had finished their ringing he would climb the rope as high as he could, and wait and watch from the bell top.

There was something about Christmas Eve that filled his heart with joy and expectation. It was as if a great and wonderful miracle were about to happen and he would be here to witness it. Tonight, however, in spite of the beauty and no matter how hard he tried to be happy, his heart was very sad.

"This is the very last Christmas Eve I will have strength to climb the rope. I shall never see this glorious sight again." Suddenly he was very cold. He legs ached and the wind nibbled at his ears. Elizer crouched low, tucking his chin between his front feet.

"I'm so tired, so tired," he whispered. "I cannot watch any longer. I am too old, too tired, too cold." He closed his eyes.

Suddenly, in the heavens a great light appeared. It fell from a star, which was beautiful beyond imagination. Warm golden beams sifted down through the falling snowflakes and rested on Elizer Mouse. He felt warm, so peaceful and sleepy. It wasn't until he heard a gentle voice calling his name that he stirred and lifted his head.

In the brightness of this magnificent light his eyes could not focus clearly. His tiny heart beat wildly, but he could not run away.

Again the voice spoke to him. "Don't be afraid, Elizer, for tonight you shall know of that great miracle you have waited for lo these many years. You will not find it here. Watch and listen near the altar in the church below."

The light faded. Elizer began to shiver. He wasn't sure if it was from the cold or if he was trembling with excitement and wonder. Quickly, he scurried down the rope, down the steps and passageway, bumping his nose on the dark, stony wall in his haste. At the end of the passage, he could see the warm light of the candles flickering on the Altar.

Not a sound stirred in the little chapel. Elizer Mouse crept closer. The altar looked different! How had he not noticed it before? Someone must have made the change while he kept watch in the bell tower. The floor was covered with small mounds of hay, shining in the golden candlelight. In the center of the floor was a tiny stool and a rough kind of cradle made of logs and filled with straw. Elizer Mouse turned round and round sniffing and touching and trying to understand the meaning of it all.

Suddenly, he could hear children's voices laughing. The great doors of the chapel swung open. As fast as his old legs would carry him, he scrambled into the corner. Only his tiny dark eyes could be seen peeking from underneath the hay. From this warm hiding place he watched as the children and their parents became very quiet. They tiptoed into the chapel one by one. The older people found a seat on the back rows of wooden benches, while some of the children took their places on the very first row. They looked so clean and shiny, their eyes sparkling with excitement and a smile on every face. They made not a sound. Other children left the room and gathered in the Choir room behind the chapel. Elizer could hear them talking in muffled voices. Now and then he thought he heard someone singing. Things were happening so fast; before he could figure out one mystery, another one was unfolding.

From the side of the Altar, a grey-haired little lady entered and sat on the stool of the great organ. Elizer loved music. Every Sunday for years and years he had watched from the balcony as the Choir sang, and the organ music filled the church. When old Bishop Flarity came to the front to speak, he would always run away. Bishop Flarity had a way of clearing his throat and peering over his spectacles that made Elizer's downey hair stand on end.

Softly now, the music began to play, "Oh Little Town of Bethlehem, How still we see Thee Lie."

"What was Bethlehem?" Bishop Flarity had walked to the front of the chapel. He cleared his throat, peered over his glasses and began to speak. "Tonight, dear ones, we are gathered together in this Holy Place. We have come to hear the story of a miracle that happened so long ago and is still happening in the hearts of all God's children who have love, one for another."

When Elizer Mouse heard the word, miracle, his ears perked up and his tiny eyes opened wide in amazement. Bishop Flarity took his seat and a small boy dressed in shepherd's robe and carrying a crooked staff climbed the steps to the altar, his round face shining brightly in the candlelight. In a clear voice he began.

The night was cold – the way was far.
Three wisemen followed a heavenly star,
To Bethlehem. Bringing gifts to a royal birth.

Shepherds watched their flocks that night
And wondered at the glorious light,
While angels sang of Bethlehem and
"Peace to Men on Earth."

Suddenly a noise turned Elizer's attention to the center of the room. He had been watching the Shepherd so intently, he had not seen the other two children enter. The little boy, Joseph, dressed in a soft striped robe, leaned toward a dark-haired little girl seated on the stool.

"Don't you worry, Mary," he comforted. "God will take care of you this holy night." Mary nodded and laid her head against his shoulder.

"Silent Night, Holy Night, All is Calm, All is Bright." The beautiful words and music filled the room and the spirit of peace and love entered every heart and soul. Five little angels in white dresses and silver halos joined hands and circled around Mary and Joseph. When, at last, they stepped aside, Elizer could not believe his eyes. For there on the straw in the little cradle was the most beautiful baby he had ever seen. A light glowed around his head. His little hands moved and a soft cry passed over tiny rosebud lips. It was as if Elizer had been carried away to a strange and wonderful place. "Bethlehem," he whispered "this must be Bethlehem."

"Away in a Manger," the children sang, and they called the baby, Jesus. "Little Lord Jesus," born king to all the world.

The Shepherd continued speaking:

> *"The baby in a manger lay*
> *A holy child, upon the hay,*
> *And angels watched him while he slept*
> *And all around their silence kept.*

The wisemen came bearing gifts. The shepherds came with humble hearts. They worshipped the child and, in return, they received the greatest gift of all, the gift of peace and love for one another.

The children stood to sing their final song, "Joy to the World." It rang from the rafters of the old country church. Joy filled Elizer's heart until he was sure it would burst.

The little shepherd boy finished his poem.

> *Prince of Peace, small holy boy,*
> *Come to fill the earth with joy.*

Born this night, this tiny one
Jesus Christ, God's holy son
To love and bless us, EVERYONE.

With joyful hearts, the crowd, young and old, wished each other a "Merry Christmas" and left the chapel. Bishop Flarity snuffed out the candles, leaving the church silent and dark, except for a tiny lamp glowing on the wall above the manger.

Elizer Mouse had not moved from his hiding place. When he was sure that he was all alone, he tipped across the floor and climbing up, peeped over the edge of the cradle. THE TINY CHILD WAS NOT THERE! WHERE HAD THEY TAKEN HIM? He wanted to gaze on his face, to touch his little hands. Tiny teardrops dribbled to the end of his whiskers and glittered in the lamplight. THIS CHILD WAS THE MIRACLE OF CHRISTMAS. At last, his dream had come true. After all these years he , ELIZER MOUSE, had witnessed it. And now, the child was gone...

In the silence of this holy night, a still small voice whispered to his heart, "Don't cry, little mouse. Let your heart be filled with joy, peace and love, "FOR LO, I AM WITH YOU ALWAYS."

DEAR LITTLE CHILD

Where are you going dear little child,
With eyes so bright and a heavenly smile?
"I'm going to live with my Father above.
He bade me to come and He gave me His love."
But how will you get there, the journeys-so Long?
Will you learn to choose wisely the right from the wrong?
"Good parents will teach me His words to obey,
In the footsteps of Jesus, I'll go all the Way."
Please may I come with you to this Glory Divine?
And He placed his little hand, trusting in mine.

A CALL FOR ME

Today…A call came just for me.
A sacred call to love and serve my brother
I prayed…but still the work seemed much too hard.
Surely Lord…Thou meant this for another.
I was afraid…but as I knelt alone beside my bed,
A voice…a gentle voice, with sweet persuasion, said,-
"Come Follow Me…one step now to show thy faith,
And then…if by thy earnest prayer, thou seekest me,
I'll give thee light to guide and keep thee safe- each day,
And lest thou fall, I'll walk beside thee All-The-Way

THE LITTLE BROWN BEAR

The Raggedy, Shaggy Brown Teddy Bear
With worn out paws and scruffy hair
Sat by himself in the old rocking chair
Forgotten by someone who once placed him there.

The twinkling lights from the stars in the sky,
Danced down through the window and into his eyes.
The smile that he wore was a perfect disguise
For the little sad heart that was lonely and wise,

How he longed for the child who once held him tight
Snuggled and hugged him and kissed him good night.
Who wasn't afraid when they blew out the light
With Teddy beside him, his world was just right.

Where were the warm sunny days "Back When"
They laughed and they played and the boy was his friend?
They shared secrets and heartaches and dreams without end.
And Teddy never Knew, "Boys grow up to be Men."

But the boy did grow up, so handsome, so tall
Dad measured his height on the old cabin wall.

And soon he was gone, with no warning at all.
While the little Bear waited through Summer and Fall.

He patiently waited through Winter and Spring
Flowers bloomed in the meadow and robins took wing
He heard in the wind, a most wonderful thing.
A familiar voice, that made his heart sing.

Then into the cabin his friend came with pride.
A beautiful wife stood close by his side
In a blanket of blue, a sweet Baby cried
And the little Bear's heart just melted inside.
Grandma and Grandpa were so filled with Joy
Home now, at last, came their wandering Boy.
And new daughter and grandchild To Love and enjoy
They gave to the Baby, a shiny new toy.

The wee Baby turned his head to the side
He was hungry and frightened and wanted to hide
The more they hushed him, the harder he cried
And he wouldn't stop crying, whatever they tried.

Till his Father reached down in the old rocking chair
And took in his arms the Little Brown Bear
All Raggedy and Shaggy and torn here and there.
He Knew that his dear little child would not care.

So Lifting the Blanket he tucked him right in.
Baby knew in a moment the Bear was his friend
He smiled as Bear's fuzzy nose tickled his chin
And The Cycle of Love, began over again.

THE GIFT

Christmas is a time of miracles, wonderful beyond imagination. They come into the lives of some, bright and beautiful, to be seen by all and never to be forgotten. To others they come silently, unexpectedly, precious and merciful, changing the heart forever. It is of one such miracle that I write this story.

High on a rocky ledge of the Appalachian Mountains stood an old log cabin. For fifty years it had weathered icy blizzards, howling winds and rain, the foggy mists of early springtime, and the hot summer sun. Still, it stood sturdy and strong, protecting the family of Jess and Mary Bolton, who lived within its walls.

Up until a year ago I would have said that it was one of the happiest places on the face of the earth. Jess Bolton had lived in this same cabin as a young boy and had stayed on after his Pa and Ma died ten years ago. At nineteen he had married Mary Morgan, his childhood sweetheart, and brought her to live with him there. She bore him two healthy sons. The firstborn was Jacob who took after Jess in both looks and personality. Red-haired, blue-eyed, "jokeful," freckle-faced Jacob had a happy contagious laugh that echoed down the mountainside into the lush green valley below. Then there was Ben. He was dark and blue eyed like his mother and his grandmother Morgan. Ben was a quiet boy and quick to learn. He followed Jacob everywhere his four-year-old legs would allow, except down the mountain to school, though he had tried that too, more than once. Ben loved music and would stop his play to listen to Mary sing, or Jess play his mandolin.

I think Mary loved this mountain home more than anyone. She could hardly wait each spring for the wild flowers and sweet shrubs to bloom, and gathered armfuls to fill the three cabin rooms with purple, pink, and golden blossoms. She loved the sounds of the birds in the first light of dawn and sang as she went about the chores of the day. There was cooking and sewing to be done, with what little money Jess could provide from his work at the sawmill. She carried water from the mountain streams to wash. Little Ben tagged along behind stepping his bare toes into every drop of water that splashed from the heavy buckets. He darted in and out of the tall pines, hiding and shooting at imaginary Indians who lurked there.

"Come along now, Ben," Mary would coax, "Jacob will be a-comin' from school and your Pa will soon be home from the mill. There is work to do and I need a good boy to help me wash the beans and make the biscuits for supper."

Soon Jacob could be seen climbing the path up the mountainside. It was a seven-mile walk from the one-room schoolhouse in the valley. Jess would follow in a few hours, whistling along the way. He would come through the door, lift Mary in to the air, whirl her around the crude wooden table in the middle of the room, huggin' and teasin' and then settle down with the boys to hear all the happenings of the day while Mary set the meal and joined them. This was the way it was...happy, noisy, and wonderful.

Then suddenly from nowhere tragedy had struck with all its terror and heartbreak. Silence and sadness, cold and dark as a winter storm, hung heavily over the little cabin.

It had happened just a few days before Thanksgiving. Winter had come early and snow blanketed the tall pines. Early that morning Jess took down his rifle from over the fireplace. He had decided it was a good day to go a-huntin'. Nine-year-old Jacob set up a ruckus to go along, too. He loved to hunt and fish with his Pa. This time, because of a fever and sore throat, Mary had forbidden it. He lay there wrapped in one of grandmother Morgan's quilts.

"I hate it," he fussed, "I'm all wound up tighter'n one of them storybook Egyptshun mummies." Jess only laughed and bundled himself and little Benjamin out of the door. Mary hadn't wanted Ben to go along, but just because he had turned five years old a few weeks before,

14

he "lowed" he was growed up enough to go a-huntin'. Jess promised to stay only a few hours because of the bone-piercing cold, and Mary gave in.

All morning it snowed. By the early afternoon shadows fell across the deep mounds in front of the cabin. Still, they had not come home. Because he was tired of watching his Ma pace back and forth, and because the fever made him drowsy, Jacob fell asleep. Mary tried to sing as she finished the applesauce she was making, but the words would not come. She tried to sew a patch on the knee of Ben's pants, but she kept stopping to listen…listen for a sound, any sound but the crackling of the log fire in the fireplace. Then out of the night there came a heavy pounding on the door. Jacob jerked awake. From across the room Mary stared at him, wide-eyed and frightened. Who would come a-callin' so late in the evening? Neighbor folk would not venture up the mountain after dark.

"Who's thar?" Mary called through the heavy wooden door.

"It's me, Mary, Solomon Lathum."

"It's your pa's boss down at the mill," she whispered to Jacob as she pulled the latch on the door. Snow covered his jacket and boots and dumped in dirty puddles on the floor. Slowly he removed his hat, letting fall a tangled mass of coal-black hair to his shoulders.

"If you came to visit with Jess," began Mary,

"he ain't home." Solomon stared down at his boots.

"You're welcome to come and sit a spell and warm by the fire if you're a mind to wait."

Slowly Solomon began to speak. "I come all this way from old Doc Henry to bring you word, Mary. His voice strained and trembled. "Ye see, Buck James and his brother was a-huntin', too. They crossed the deep end of Willow Creek and came across your Jess and Ben. They must have tried to cross the creek there, too. The log broke and they went into the icy water. Jess' leg was pinned down by the log on some rocks. They was...they was...drowned." Solomon lifted his head. "It was a "horroful" thing and terrible." His shoulders shook and tears filled his large, grey eyes and streamed down his roughly bearded cheeks. Mary stood straight as a poker, her eyes staring in unbelief. Jacob wanted to scream, but the sound froze in his throat. A great knot twisted his stomach and he covered his head with the heavy quilt to drown out the sound of his Mother's sobbing.

For the next few days the neighbors came and went bringing food and solemn words. The funeral was held in the one little church in the valley. It was small, brown, and plain. It was the first time Jacob had been inside. Jess had not been a church goer, and Mary had given up trying to persuade him. The seats were hard and cold as the wind blew through the cracks in the door. Jacob sat close to his Mother staring at the two crude caskets. One, so big and one so small. There were no flowers to gather in the winter, so boughs of holly and crow foot draped the rough boards. Old Widow Banes sang, "The Old Rugged Cross." That's all he could remember.

A year had passed since. Mary, still quiet and very lonely, had found work down in the valley cleaning and cooking at the Guest Lodge. Jacob attended school, and afterwards walked the long road, climbed the mountain to an empty cabin, and did the chores til Mary came at sundown. He missed his Pa so much, and most of all he missed Ben, his buddy, pal, gone from him forever.

Now Thanksgiving came again. The children could hardly wait for school to close for the holiday. They bounded out of the door squealing and racing in all directions. Jacob was the last to leave. Today it was especially hard for him to begin the long journey home. His thoughts were filled with that sorrowful day a year ago. Oh how alone he felt, and how he missed the way the family used to be. He could almost hear Ben's laughter in the cold winter wind. He shuffled along the road pulling his worn jacket up under his chin and his squirrel cap down over his ears.

About four miles along, he left the path to follow a deer heading down towards Willow Creek. The path was steep and rocky under the snow. At the foot of the hill he lost sight of the deer. Tired of the hunt, he turned to follow the creek back toward the mountain when he heard a low moaning sound coming from behind a huge pile of fallen rock. He edged closer, trying to see without being seen.

There behind the largest rock lay an old man. His hair was as white as the snow on which he lay. His eyes were closed. In one wrinkled hand he held part of a broken cane. A small bundle wrapped in a square of red wool lay nearby. Jacob asked him questions about the pain and where he was a-hurtin, but the old man could not answer. It was frightening thing to see one lay so still. Jerking off his jacket, Jacob covered the old man as best he could and pulled his own squirrel cap down on the white head. Then running as fast as he could through the snow-filled forest, he made his way to old Doc Henry.

The doctor's sons came to carry the old man, and Jacob followed along behind, carrying the old man's broken cane and the strange red bundle back to Doc Henry's home.

Jacob waited till almost dark by the fire till the doctor came in to say that the old man, Mr. Sweeney, would live. He was very sick and weak, and would have to stay with the doctor unless someone could be found to care for him at his cabin back on Willow Creek. Jacob spoke right up.

"My Ma, Mrs. Bolton, could come every morning and stop every afternoon on her way to and from the village. I could come after school and stay til my Ma comes. We could make his meals and see to him til he's better."

And so it was to be. Mary Bolton and Jacob and old Doc Henry nursed Mr. Sweeney til his old bones found new strength. The old man loved Jacob, and one day when he was feeling better, he had the boy bring to his bedside the small red bundle that Jacob had carried for him. Opening it, Jacob's eyes were to behold a wonderful sight. Inside were twelve beautiful figures, magnificently hand carved in detail. There was Mary and Joseph looking down at the baby Jesus. There were three tall wisemen bearing gifts, a donkey, a camel, a shepherd, two sheep, and an angel with long flowing robes. Jacob had never heard the story of the birth of Jesus, how he came to be born in Bethlehem, or of the innkeeper turning them away in the chilly night, only to call them back and at last give them room in a stable. As the old man told the story of the wisemen and the shepherds and the glorious angels singing in the starlit heavens, Jacob's eyes glowed and sparkled as brightly as any star. He listened and held each piece, one after the other. The story did not end there.

The old man told also how Jesus died on the cross so that all men could be forgiven and live with Him and their very own family in heaven. As a special gift, he gave to Jacob the figures of Mary, Joseph, and baby Jesus. He would carve new ones to finish his set, the set he had been carrying to sell at the Guest Lodge when he had fallen in the snow. Jacob was thrilled with his new gift. He begged the old man to tell the wonderful story again and again at each visit.

On Christmas Eve, most of the folks in the valley gathered at the little church. Mary had stopped as usual to check on old Mr. Sweeney, and after much persuasion from Jacob, the three of them walked through the cold night air to join the others.

There were candles in the church windows along with sprigs of holly. The altar area was bare, except for the choir, such as it was. Mrs. Emily Hawkins singing the high melody, and Solomon Lathum bringing up the base, sounded lovely tonight. They sang, "Little Town of Bethlehem," and "Silent Night," and the children sang, "Away in a Manager." Angels in overalls and cotton feed sack dresses, smiling in the candlelight, Jacob wondered if his Ma knew the story about the baby Jesus.

The service ended, and the people filed out into the crisp, cold air. Stars in the heavens were beautiful, sparkling and glittering against a deep blue velvet sky. The three walked hand in hand along the frozen roadway, when suddenly Jacob stopped. "Ma, you go on with Mr. Sweeney to the cabin. I forgot something. I'll be right along."

Before she could stop him, he hurried away into the darkness, back to the Church. It was empty now, but the starlight streamed in through

20

the narrow windows. Jacob tiptoed to the altar, and kneeling there in the soft light, he thanked God for the baby Jesus. He loved him with all his heart, and asked him to please take "ceer" of his Pa and little brother, Ben, till he could come to them. Reaching into his pocket, he lifted out the figures of Mary, Joseph and the baby, and carefully placed them on the altar. They would be there for someone else who needed to know of the great miracle of love. He closed the doors of the old church and smiled up into the starlight. It was as if a great weight had been lifted from his small shoulders. He wasn't sad at leaving his treasured gift, for he had received a gift far more precious, a gift of lasting love, AND HE WOULD NEVER AGAIN WALK ALONE.

AMANDA'S TOES

"Amanda." The name suited her perfectly. It was a happy name, full of sparkle and imagination. Her grandmother said it was a "wee bit of the Irish" that touched her blonde hair with red and put the sparkle in her eyes. She had an easy laugh, the kind that seemed to trickle all the way down to her toes, and that's important because...that is what this story is all about - Amanda's toes. But, let us begin at the beginning.

When Amanda was born, it was a proud and happy day. Her mother touched her tiny face and hands and whispered, "someday you will grow up and be very beautiful." Her brothers, Sean and Clinton, were sure that she would be a great athlete, maybe a tennis star, or play women's basketball. Her father wrapped the pink blanket close around her, held her closely, and waltzed her across the room humming softly as he rocked her in his arms. Maybe it was the music, or perhaps the swaying rhythm of his steps as he carried her to her crib. But there was no mistaking

22

it. There were Amanda's toes up out of the blanket, wiggling happily in the air. I think in her tiny heart she knew at that very moment that someday she would dance.

As time passed, Amanda grew tall and thin. Heavenly Father sent a little sister Rosemary, to keep her company. After all, brothers did not always understand "girl talk." Rosemary would share her room and her dreams and ask her a million questions. Best of all, she was her friend. Whenever they listened to music, it was always the same. A very strange thing happened. First, a dreamy look came into Amanda's eyes. A happy smile tiptoed across her lips. Then her toes began to wiggle, wiggle till up on tiptoe, ever so gracefully, she would whirl and twirl, pirouette, arabesque, and releve until the music stopped.

At school Amanda learned many new things. The more she studied and the harder she worked, the smarter she became. She helped her mother with the housework and the cooking. She learned to embroider, too.

One day something wonderful happened. Her parents asked if she would like to take ballet lessons. Amanda was so happy she could hardly wait to begin the lessons. She knew that her mother and father would have to work very hard to pay for the lessons, so she tried all the harder to learn the difficult steps. Her teacher, Miss Bailey, was very impressed.

At the first ballet recital the whole family came. They were very proud of her. Even her grandfather and grandmother and aunt and uncles who lived way out in Salt Lake City, Utah, were excited when they heard about the lovely performance. Her teacher was so pleased with the recital that she began to plan a very special ballet program for the Christmas holidays.

Three months before Christmas the dance studio was buzzing with activity. There were costumes to make, scenery to paint, and difficult steps to practice, practice, practice. Each child was given an important part, and each child took his part very seriously, especially Amanda. She was chosen to dance the part of the <u>Snow Fairy</u>.

As the time drew near, people in the neighborhood bought tickets and waited anxiously for the appointed day. However, there was in the city, one small child who was not anxious about the ballet or anything else. Her name was Martha Williams, and she was six years old. Martha's legs had been injured in a terrible accident the year before. She could not walk. She spent her days in a wheelchair, watching the other children run and play. She wanted so much to join in their games. The doctor said it was possible if she would exercise and practice hard learning to walk again. Martha tried. It was so painful that she decided it was easier just to watch. She was sad and lonely, and had almost forgotten how to smile. Her mother and father bought tickets to the ballet program. They hoped that the music and the happy children would cheer their little daughter.

On the day before the program, there was a grand dress rehearsal. The children practiced in their costumes and were allowed to take them home for a final pressing. As the rehearsal ended, the children laughed and shouted goodbye to each other. They held the precious costumes ever so tightly as they hurried away.

Amanda and her mother left the studio talking excitedly. Amanda held her dress and her new white satin dancing slippers. She could hardly wait to show Rosemary, Sean, Clinton and her father the beautiful costume.

It was so late when they arrived home that she decided to wait until after dinner. She carried the precious bundle to her bedroom. As she spread the costume across the bed she discovered, in one horrible moment, that one of the lovely white satin dancing slippers was missing. She looked under the bed, in the hall, on the front walk, and down the street all the way to the corner. The slipper was nowhere in sight. Father made a second trip to the corner to double check, and mother tried to comfort her. "Maybe it is back at the studio," she said. "I will go and look for it tomorrow morning. I am sure it must be there."

Amanda could not eat a bite. A worried look settled over her forehead and stayed there all through dinner. Amanda began to clear away the dirty dishes from the table when the front doorbell rang. It was Mrs. Harrison who lived down the street. She handed something to father as she spoke. "My puppy, Rags, brought this home. I was sure it must be Amanda's." Father thanked her and closed the door.

He turned slowly, and there in his hand was the lost slipper, or at least what was left of it. It was wet and dirty, and the once lovely white satin ribbons were in tangled shreds. Worst of all, right in the toe was a big hole. Amanda took the slipper tenderly in her own small hands. Her eyes filled with tears and trickled down between the freckles on her face to her chin. She could not speak. The great lump in her throat was too painful. Even mother's hug and promise to try and mend the slipper did not make the lump go away. She cried herself to sleep.

The next day mother really did try to work a miracle on the shoe. She washed it, added new ribbon, but that gaping hole in the toe was a "thing to reckon with." It was at last mended with a patch cut from one of mother's old white satin nighties. But the patch was dull and yellowed with age. When Amanda tried it on, it pinched her big toe something awful. "It will just have to do," said mother. "There isn't time for anything else."

That evening Amanda wore her white fairy dress. It was downy soft and had tiny silver sparkles on the skirt. The soft curls of her hair were caught up in a pony tail and fastened to a bright silver crown on her head. Her mother looked at her and beamed. She was remembering when she had held her in her little pink blanket and whispered that she would grow up and be very beautiful. Now her mother's dreams had come true.

Amanda's brothers tried to cheer her. Rosemary had helped her to dress and was simply bursting with excitement. Father held her coat and gave her a big hug, but nothing helped. Amanda was SAD as she pulled on her boots and carried her dancing slippers to the car.

Backstage at the auditorium the children hurried about making last-minute adjustments. Amanda sat, one shoe on and one shoe off, staring at the toe of her new white leotard. She knew that her teacher and all of the children were depending on her. Her own family would be counting on her to do her best. BUT HOW COULD ANYONE EXPECT HER TO DANCE WITH THAT BIG, UGLY PATCH PINCHING HER BIG TOE?

Amanda's heart was heavy as she tied the bow of her slipper and joined the other children, center stage, behind the curtain. The auditorium was packed to capacity, not a single empty seat. Even little Martha Williams was in her place in the front row. Miss Bailey was making the introduction. The lights lowered, the people hushed, the curtain rose, all was silent.

The music, the <u>beautiful</u> music began to play. A soft, dreamy look floated over Amanda's face. A tiny smile tiptoed across her lips, and miracle of miracles, her toes began to wiggle. She closed her eyes and suddenly felt as if she were all alone, high in the sky, whirling and twirling with thousands of sparkling snowflakes. She was dancing over the snowy meadows and frozen rivers, beneath crystal branches in a winter wonderland of light and magic. Her feet were as light as a fairy's breath as she danced and danced til the music slowed.

Then, bending low, her graceful fingers barely touching the floor, she assumed her last lovely pose. The music stopped. The crowd was silent. Then a great roar of applause filled the auditorium. The crowd was on its feet. clapping and cheering. Miss Bailey had tears in her eyes, and the faces of Amanda's family were glowing with pride.

Little Martha Williams was laughing and clapping her small hands. She hugged her mother and whispered, with eyes sparkling, "I am going to practice every day until I can walk. Someday I want to dance like the Snow Fairy." And that is just what she did. Martha worked hard at her exercises, in spite of the pain until she could walk, run, and yes, even dance.

Amanda never knew about little Martha Williams. She only knew that she was nearly exploding with happiness. As she knelt beside her bed, she thanked Heavenly Father for the wonderful, magical, miracle night. In the years to come, she would dance in many lovely satin slippers, but this little raggedy shoe with its yellowed patch would always be her favorite. She tucked it under her pillow and climbed into bed.

She felt very tired, and was soon fast asleep. A huge silver moon sent it's beams tiptoeing across the lawn, through the bedroom window, and rested across the foot of her bed. In the stillness of her sleep, Amanda's eyelashes fluttered. A sweet smile turned up the corners of her mouth, and up from under the blankets, moving ever so slowly in the moonlight, were Amanda's wonderful toes.

OUT OF THE STORM

A great north wind howled it's way down the canyon, wrapped itself around Sarah Jenkin's little cabin and shook it til the windows rattled and the walls trembled in its grasp. It was the beginning of a heavy winter storm. Sarah Jenkins had lived through many winter storms, but this one was different. This time, for the first time in nearly 70 years, she would be completely alone. Sarah pulled the old rocking chair closer to the fireplace. The wind outside snatched the warmth of the fire up the chimney, but the firelight danced on the hearth and on the cabin walls. The flame in the oil lamp flickered, spreading erie shadows over the old wooden table in the center of the room.

"I should git me to bed," she thought, but it was cozy here in the old rocker, wrapped in a quilt she had made so many years ago when fingers were nimble and it was easy to sew. Her hands were wrinkled now, and the fingers bent and crooked as the weathered old pines on the cliff above the cabin.

She reached up carefully and loosened the pins at the back of her hair. It fell long and silvery white about her face and shoulders. It had been a lovely dark brown in her youth, when she had first come to this little valley with her new doctor husband. He, Doctor William Jenkins, had been the first young doctor to leave the big city of Ashland,Kentucky, and move to Greenwood Valley. Some said he was foolish, but they were not afraid of the wilderness. He was full of energy and love for the people, and understanding of their problems. Sarah had come willingly away from her family and friends to make a new life here with her beloved William. They bought a small farm, 20 acres, and built a cabin. In a little while they added several horses, two cows, some pigs and chickens.

William worked hard to get to know the people round about. They were a clannish bunch, not easily given to making friendly conversation. They were superstitious and full of pride. It was not an easy task William set for himself. Those who would let themselves come to know him, over the years learned to love and trust him.

Sarah loved him, too. They had wanted children, especially Sarah. She spent so much time alone while William made his regular calls on patients. This blessing was not to be. Three times she had given birth to a precious baby girl. Three times they had come early and were not strong enough to live more than a few days. With aching hearts, they had buried them in a lovely little grove near the mountain, sweet little Jenny, Kathleen, and Sarah Ann. In the springtime the wild roses grew there with the columbine.

Sarah thought of them now, three little mounds under the heavy falling snow and beneath wild winds. If only the girls had lived, they would be grown now, beautiful and full of laughter. Grandchildren would fill the cabin. How she would have loved them all. Somehow, she and Will had endured their loss. They had comforted and blessed each other's lives until just before Thanksgiving this year. William came down with the flu, and he died so suddenly. It was as if her whole world slipped silently away with him. The loneliness was almost too much to bear.

Tonight was Christmas Eve. But for Sarah, there was no outward sign except for a small wooden manger on the mantle. "Christmas needs a family, gifts in purdy red ribbons and music...yes, music," nodded Sarah with a smile. In a low, sweet voice, in the midst of a howling storm, she softly sang "Silent Night." It might have been the lateness of the hour or the steady creak of the rocking chair that caused a peaceful sleep to tiptoe in and hush the song. Then, suddenly, the silence was shattered by a loud pounding on the cabin door. The sound of it so startled Sarah she nearly toppled the chair as she struggled to free her feet from the quilt around her ankles.

It was only a few steps across the floor to the door. The force of the wind and the snow stung her cheeks as she swung it open. There, braced against the gale, stood Charlie Webb, owner of the general store in town. His hat was pulled down over his brow and his collar was pulled up, leaving only a red nose and squinting eyes for Sarah to recognize.

"Charlie, you sceert me half to death," shouted Sarah, barely audible above the storm.

"I shore am sorry to wake ye so late, Sarey, but I need your help somethin' fearce. I got a young woman and little girl in my wagon. They came on the train this afternoon. I promised to drive 'um up to Cobblecreek, but the storm bogged us down. We had trouble crossing the stream. The woman is havin' lots of pain. I think it's near time for her baby. Can ye' take 'um in for the night?" Sarah was wide awake now and as was her way, took charge.

"Hurry, git 'um in quick outter the cold," she hollered over her shoulder as she hurried to turn down the big bed in the back corner of the cabin. Several quilts and blankets were quickly made into a soft pallet by the fireplace. Charlie returned with a tiny girl wrapped in an old woolen blanket. Her frightened eyes looked deep into Sarah's, filled with tears, but she made no sound. Charlie laid her on the pallet near the fire and hurried out again into the storm. In almost no time, Sarah found a warm flannel shirt that had been William's, cut off half the sleeves, and dressed the child in the makeshift nightie, hanging her wet clothing over a chair to dry. She bundled her under the warm blankets.

Meanwhile, Charlie carried in the child's mother. She was very young. Her face was nearly as white as the snow that covered her long dark hair and thin cloth coat. Her lips were so cold they could hardly form the words, "I'm so sorry, so sorry to be such a bother."

"There now," comforted Sarah, "I'm glad yore here. I'll have 'ya warm as can be in jist a minute." She turned to Charlie. He was standing by the fire in a puddle of melted snow. "Charlie, I know it's cold, but I got to ask 'ya to sleep in the barn. There's straw a-plenty, and it's tight against the wind." She handed him blankets, a dry shirt and overalls, and some cornbread and beans left over from supper.

"Thankey, Sarey," he said, "I'll be fine now." He hurried out to shelter his horses and himself in the barn.

It was a difficult chore getting the woman out of her wet clothing and into a warm flannel nightgown. She was very heavy with child and in so much pain. Sarah gently dried her hair and tucked her into the large feather bed. The young woman tried to explain.

"My name is Jenny Stone, and that's my little girl, Mary Kathleen," she said, pointing to the child sleeping peacefully now on the pallet. "We are on our way to Cobblecreek to find Samuel and Mary Stone. They're my husband's people." Her eyes were suddenly sad and serious. "My husband was killed in a railroad accident last month. The Railroad gave me free passage here to find his folks. I wrote to his folks asking if we could come." She paused, "I got no one else to turn to. I ain't heard a word from them, so I thought maybe my letter got lost. I was hoping we could stay with them till I could earn some money for a little place of our own."

Sarah knew of Samuel and Mary Stone. Will had treated them often. Two years ago, Samuel died suddenly from a heart attack. Mary died last winter of pneumonia. She couldn't tell Jenny this, not tonight, not on Christmas Eve. Besides, there were more important things to attend to. She asked about the baby.

"Well, my time ain't til the middle of January, but the pains started on the train. Then there was all that joltin' around in the wagon. I think the baby's a-comin early." Jenny tried not to show how very frightened she was, but fear could not hide from Sarah. She knew it well. Like an old enemy, it was tearing away at half-healed scars from long ago. She patted Jenny's hand and turned away to set a large pot of water on the stove to boil.

"Don't you fret now, child. My husband was a fine doctor before he died. He delivered lots and lots of healthy younguns. He let me come along with him sometimes and help. If the baby comes tonight, we'll be ready. You try and rest. I gotta' git more logs for the fire." Taking her coat and shawl from the nail by the door, she hurried out into the freezing darkness. The snow was deep, making it difficult to move. She stumbled toward the wood pile behind the cabin.

It wasn't the storm or the driving wind that tormented her mind and heart this night. It was something far greater and more dangerous. Fear was a terrible enemy to face. Between an old shed and the huge pile of logs, she found a narrow space to duck into out of the icy wind. She bowed her head and dropped to her knees in the snow.

"Oh Lord," she began. "It's me, Sarah, a-prayin' to 'ya for help. 'Ya know, when Will was here, I weren't afraid at birthin' time. I mostly stood by whilst you and Will did all the work. I was so proud at the gift you gave him. But Will is gone from me now and I got to bring this new baby into the world all by myself. I'm thinkin', Lord, of my dear babies buried out there under the snow. Please, don't let this baby die, Lord, I'm a-beggin' ya'. It must have been a night jist like this so long ago, when your own dear Mama was so tired and sceered and no one wanted to give you room to be born. But you came into the world healthy and beautiful, bringing joy and love and mercy to everyone. Lord, I'm a-prayin' to ya' now to take these old hands of mine in yores and guide this little child through the Valley of Death and bring him into the light. Make him strong and healthy to live for good, I pray. Amen."

She stood quietly for a moment and then gathering logs for the fire, she hurried back towards the house. As she neared the porch, she could hear Jenny scream her name. The time had come, ready or not. She must have faith and do her best.

Sarah scrubbed, comforted Jenny, and prepared all that she could for the birth. The next few hours passed quickly. It seemed as if the fire and the lamp burned brighter, filling the room with the necessary light for the heavenly task. A feeling of calm overshadowed Sarah, and she eased the pain of the new mother-to-be. Finally at long last, in the wee hours of the morning, a tiny boy child was born. Sarah spanked him gently and a loud healthy cry filled the cabin. She could hardly believe her eyes...before she could wrap him properly, a second child was being born. This time, a little girl, smaller, but at far as Sarah could tell, she too was healthy and strong. She washed them, dressed them in little gowns from the chest of things she had made so long ago, and laid them close to Jenny. Too exhausted to speak, Jenny smiled up thankfully. The light in her eyes would warm Sarah for years to come. They were safe now and ready for sleep.

Sarah settled down again in the old rocker, wrapped the quilt about her knees, and closed her eyes. "I thank thee, Lord, I thank thee, Lord," she whispered, again and again.

No one noticed that the wind had stopped; the storm had passed. A beautiful silver moon was shining down upon the snow. "Silent Night, Holy Night;" all was right in Sarah's world.

Jenny and Mary Kathleen, and the twins, little William and Sarah Ann, stayed on with Sarah Jenkins. They loved and took care of each other until Sarah went to join William in heaven at the age of 93. They were an answer to a prayer from a lonely heart... a blessed family, born out of the storm on Christmas Eve.

GRANDMOTHER'S PRAYER

Grandmother sat in her favorite chair.
I sat on my stool at her knee.
"It is time, she said, for our Evening Prayer,
Come, kneel down here child, with me."

I could tell by her voice that she knew God was there.
She called Him, Dear Father, above.
And thanked Him for patiently hearing our prayer
And the comfort that comes from His love.

There were tears on her cheeks that spilled down on my hand,
When she whispered, "Oh Father, I pray,
Forgive me and help me to follow thy plan.
I was selfish and angry, today."

She asked for His guidance, His comfort and care,
For each loved one, for stranger and friend.
And promised to yield as His will be done.
In the name of Dear Jesus, Amen.

I felt peaceful and safe, loved and protected,
That night as I learned about prayer.
While a STILL SMALL VOICE whispered His message,
"If you ask, I will ALWAYS be there."

When Angels Sing

The night was bitter cold. The heavy winter winds moaned their way through the cedar trees at the corner of the house and piled high the snow beside the garden wall. I felt angry at myself as I pulled my old grey wool coat from the closet. Why had I left the last and most important gift of all, for it was Papa's, until such a cold and wintery night?

I had saved every extra penny, stuffing it into a little brown felt pouch in the pocket of my old grey coat. It had not been easy to save since Mama went to Heaven. She had been so good at it...always making sure there was enough of everything. Now, it was up to me. "Well," I thought, "at least it won't be so hard." I knew just exactly the gift I wanted to buy. I had picked them out several months ago at Mr. Burton's department store. I had worked so hard and watched the money grow, until now the pouch was nearly full.

Wrapping a warm woolen scarf around my head, I hurried out into the night. It was just a short walk into the village. Tonight, it seemed to be especially long as the wind whipped the stinging snow across my face. The lights of the village soon came into view. I picked up the pace to a slow run, when suddenly, my ankle struck against something hard beneath the snow, sending me sprawling. The pain was only sharp for a moment. I managed to pull myself up, dusting away the cold flakes and feeling ever so embarrased, even though there was no one there to witness my clumsiness. I hurried on.

The village was alive and bustling with busy people, rushing everywhere, in and out, up and down the streets. Colored lights swayed overhead in the wind. There were children slowing and stopping to gaze with wonder into the lovely Christmas windows of the shops, then being pulled or pushed along gently by busy parents. In my own heart, I could almost hear Mama's dear voice saying, "Hurry along now, Emily, we have so much to do before Papa gets home."

Mr. Burton's department store was one of the largest stores in the valley. It was crowded now with late shoppers and it was hard to move quickly. I managed to press forward towards the back of the store until at last I could see Papa's Gift. They were so beautiful, a pair of heavy brass bookends gleamed in the warm light. They were sailing ships. Papa had been a captain of a fishing boat in his younger years. I never tired of hearing the wonderful stories he could tell of his adventures at sea. I touched the shiny surface, running my fingers down the sail. They were magnificient!

I felt in my pocket for the money pouch. IT WAS GONE! It was gone, but WHERE? The shock raced down to the pit of my stomach and I could feel myself trembling as I searched every corner of the pocket. It was not there. I stared at the bookends not really seeing them through the tears. My mind raced backwards over the events of the last hour. I must go back and look for it.

My legs carried me out of the store and through the slippery streets, but my mind and heart were somewhere far beyond, praying, "Oh please, Heavenly Father, help me to find the money for Papa."

It was hard to see in the darkness between the street lamps, but my eyes searched everywhere. Then, like a miracle, at least it seemed like a miracle to me, I saw the place where I had fallen earlier on my way to the village, a large hollowed-out space in the snow. There, on the edge of it lay the little brown pouch, the precious money still inside. Clutching it tightly, and whispering a "thank you" to Heavenly Father, I raced back to the village. It was closing time and I hoped I would not be too late.

Near the entrance of the store I suddenly noticed a young boy. He had not been there when I had entered the store earlier. Around him in neat piles were bundles of holly and pine gathered from the nearby woods. "Come, buy my holly," he called. "It will make you feel happy on Christmas." His worn cap was pulled down to his ears, but was much too small to cover them. His sweater was ragged and full of holes, but he smiled at each person that passed. And pass they did, right by him without stopping on their way.

I hurried into the store, hoping against hope I would still be in time for the gift. My heart sang! There were the bookends, just as I had left them. Picking them up, I hurried to the clerk at the far end of the counter. I looked down. But instead of the beautiful sailing ships, I seemed only to see a face looking back at me from the shiny brass…the face of a smiling boy, cold and shivering in thin, ragged clothing. Suddenly the bookends felt hard and heavy in my hands. My heart stopped singing and pained me as I placed the bookends back on the counter and moved away, not knowing at that moment what to do. I only knew I could not buy them for Papa now. The little boy's face would always be there looking back at me. As I made my way to the front of the store, I found myself stopping in front of a counter piled high with warm woollen sweaters. The sign read, "Two Sweaters for the Price of One; A Late Christmas Special." I quickly picked out a bright red one with a high neck and a grey one for Papa. It would suit him perfectly. The clerk wrapped them for me in bright holiday paper, I rushed from the store to find the boy.

Thank goodness he was still there. As I ran over to him, he quickly held out a bundle of fresh holly, thinking I was a paying customer. I shook my head and handed him the package.

"It's for you," I said, "Merry Christmas!" He stared at me for a long moment, as if he could not believe the words I spoke. Then, quickly he opened the gift. The light of all the stars of heaven shone in his face as he clutched the warm sweater to him.

"It is jist what I needed," he almost shouted at me. "Come, oh please come with me." He gathered the holly and pine into an old wagon and pulled me gently by the hand.

Suddenly I was racing down the street. Me, a strange boy, and a rickety wagon rumbled and clattered through the nearly empty village streets. We rounded a corner and at the far end of the street, I saw him, a little boy much smaller than the first. His brown hair was nearly covered by a large knit hat and he wore an old flannel shirt rolled up at the sleeves to protect him against the cold.

"David, David! Wait til you see! I have a present for you. David is my little brother," he said smiling up at me, when we finally came to a stop in front of the child. "I gotta look after him now. 'Weeze all alone except for my Grampaw." He pushed the package into David's arms, hardly able to stand still for the excitement. "Open it! It's for you!"

Slowly the child opened the bundle, the bright paper dropping to the icy ground. He stared wonderingly down at it for a moment before pulling the warm, bright red sweater over his head and down, the older boy helping to shape it around his shoulders. It hung long, almost to his knees, and covered his hands to the tip of his fingers.

"It'll keep you warm, and it looks great." David laughed too, jumping up and down and running his fingers over the warm wool.

Almost as suddenly, the tiny child stopped and stood very still. It was then I saw his face clearly for the first time. His clear blue eyes were filled with tears that tumbled down his cheeks, and his tiny chin quivered as he spoke. "Matthew, you is the best brother in the whole world. I love you so much!" He threw his arms around the older boy's neck.

I left them there, the two of them. The snow swirled around them in the warm light of the street lamp. I was sure in my heart they were no longer cold, as the spirit of love filled their hearts.

As I turned and made my way toward home, I too was warm. My heart was singing again, this time for the right reason. I could almost hear angels singing somewhere in the heavens above me. From out of the darkness I remembered a passage I had read in one of Papa's books. It said, "the quality of mercy is not strained. It droppeth as the gentle rain from heaven upon the place be- neath. It is twice blessed. It blesseth him that giveth, and him that receiveth." This time I understood its meaning. As I neared home, the snow was falling gently and the wind seemed to whisper, "LOVE ONE ANOTHER."

Love Remembered

A slow steady rain washed over the red brick sidewalk and gathered in puddles in all the low places. Ellen Grayson hurriedly walked between them as she entered the old Cedarville Hospital in the small town of Westbrook, Virginia. She took the elevator to the third floor and walked quietly down the long empty corridor in search of Room 319. A nurse left her station at the end of the hall and met her at the entrance to the room. Taking her gently by the arm, the Nurse led her a few steps away from the door. "You must be Ellen, Anna Brewer's daughter. I am Mrs. Walcott. The Dr. told me you were coming. I wanted to speak with you before you went in to visit your mother." Her soft grey eyes were kind but the words she spoke were as cold as steel and pierced Ellen to the very heart. "Your Mother has completely lost her eyesight, now. It has been poor these last few years, you know. Now because of her illness and the surgery she has also lost her hearing and worse - she seems to have lost her will to live. I am sure she won't know you when you visit her. Her friends have come so many of them, but it is no use. She whispers, "Thank you" when she is cared for. Most of the time she lies there, so still; so quiet. I'm so sorry, you have come such a long way to visit her. I will be at the Nurses Station if you need me. She turned and walked away. Ellen stood, staring into the room. The cold grey light of the November morning tiptoed in through the window and settled over the one small bed and the tiny, white haired woman lying upon it. Oh Why! Why did I wait so long to vist mama? It had been seven long years since Papa died and she had made the long trip from California to Virginia, to visit her. She had meant to visit every year but something always got in the way. The children were sick, or the old car needed repair. David, her husband lost his job for awhile and there was no money. One excuse followed another. Yesterday, when the Doctor had called about her mother's surgery, Ellen came right away, on the very first plane. Now, she had finally come, only to hear that it was too late. She had waited too long. How could she tell Mama how very much she loved her and from now on she would always take care of her? How could she make her understand? Tears welled up in Ellen's eyes as she turned her face to the wall. "Oh Dear Father in Heaven." The strange words came suddenly and fell away into silence. It has been so many years since Ellen had prayed about anything. She began again in a soft whisper. "Oh Father, Please help me. I know I have not always stayed close and followed thy ways, but now I need you so. Please help Mama to know I am here with her and that I love her, with all my heart. Help me to make her understand. And then the words came no more. They were swallowed up somewhere in that deep aching hole inside. But the tears came and she was not ashamed. After a few minutes, Ellen gained control, wiped her eyes and walked to the side of the bed, not sure what to do next. The light in the room had changed. A small ray of sunshine fell across the older woman's face. Suddenly, Ellen was remembering things from so long ago. Things that had been forgotten with the busy passing of time. She remembered how as a small child she had worried about a tiny dimple-like indentation on the tip of her nose. Her Mother would tease her and touch the dimple with the tip of her finger and say," that is where an angel kissed you." It is your own special beauty spot." She also remembered how frightened she had been of her first grade teacher, Miss Pogorelskin. Her Mother, had walked with her each morning and as they neared the school, mama would always squeeze her hand. It was not just an ordinary squeeze. It was a special secret message between the two of them – two short squeezes and one long one - meaning "I Love You!" It had given her the courage she needed to face the day.

Ellen was smiling now. God had answered her prayer. She leaned over the bed, softly touched her mother's nose and kissed her on the tip of it. She took her frail hand in her own and gave it the secret squeeze - two short and one very long one. For a moment Anna Brewer lay very still. Then slowly she placed her hand on Ellens. Suddenly she was smiling - a glorious smile! "Oh Ellen is it you?" I knew in my heart you would come. Heavenly Father told me so. If it really is you, squeeze my hand again." Ellen repeated the secret squeeze. Suddenly they were both laughing and hugging all at the same time. Neither of them were aware of Nurse Walcott standing in the doorway, weeping with them as she witnessed a miracle of Love Remembered.

A Widow's Might

The little mountain village of Greenwood, Kentucky was hardly visible on the map. There was a Church, a filling station, Charley Day's General Store – and Sister Bessie Thompson sold handmade dresses to those ladies what had money to buy um. Very few visitors ever came to Greenwood and those families born there, never ventured far away. At the far end of the Village – high up the mountain path, there lived an elderly widow. Her name was Sarah Beam. She had been alone for almost twenty years now since the death of her beloved husband. She kept busy in her little house and yard and came down the mountain on Saturdays to the General Store and on Sunday to Church. She had a daughter, a Son-in-law and two beautiful grandaughters who lived in the next village but they seldom came to visit. Oh! how she missed them.

One cold winter morning widow Beam sat in her rocker in front of the fireplace mending a hole in the elbow of her favorite sweater, when there came a knock at her door. It was the new Bishop. His arms held a large box. He smiled at her as he stamped the snow from his heavy boots. "Storm coming in, It's a mite too cold for you to go trampin down to the store. Thought you could use a few things, he said." "My Goodness, didn't he know I been trampin through snow deeper'n this all my life?" She smiled with a twinkle in her eye. "Come in Bishop, she said, have a cup of cocoa with me." They talked for nearly an hour. "I'm worred bout the folks in the village, he told her. Some is sick – Some is out of work – and got nothing much to eat. I'm worried <u>most bout those what just don't seem to care anymore.</u> They've stopped comin to Church. After the Bishop left, Sarah sat for a long time thinking about all the things he had said. There must be something she could do. Finally she knelt by the side of the chair and asked the Dear Lord for His help. Well, it was as if a large flood gate opened wide and the ideas POURED through her mind. She knew just where to begin. Emptying the box the Bishop had brought, she found a chicken, some vegetables and flour. All day she worked refilling the box. She made a large kettle of Chicken soup, Sugar Cookies and on an on till the box was spilling over. The next morning Bright and Early, Sarah tied the box to an old sled with a piece of rope and carefully made her way down the mountain. The wind was cold and sharp. She pulled her woolen scarf tight about her head and singing a merry song she hoped the storm would hold till her work was finished. Sarah visited house after house, leaving soup-for the Hawkins family – Brother Hawkins out of work – eight children to feed. There was yarn and a book for Sister Wayne who broke her leg and had to stay in bed. The most difficult call was to Old Brother Jessop. He had lost his wife the year before. He was lonely, angry and not very receptive to meddlin neighbors. But, Sarah had a plan. She asked him if he would help her with a birthday gift for her grandchild. She told him she knew how good he was at whittlin things. How he was an Artist-Sure and true. At these favorable words a faint suggestion of a smile crossed Brother Jessop's lips. Sarah had torn a picture from an old magazine of a little miniature rocking horse. Could you whittle me this – no hurry – don't need it till late Summer? I'll be glad to pay ya for it. Her eyes pleaded so…he couldn't rightly refuse. I won't promise, he said softly, but maybe I could give it a try.

It was nearly sundown by the time the last sugar cookie and hug were given away and Sarah returned to her home. Too tired and weary to eat, she made a fire in the fireplace and settled in the old rocker to rest. She wasn't sure if the wonderful warmth she was feeling came from the fire or from somewhere down deep inside.

Before the Spring Sunshine melted the last of the Winter Snow and the flowers began to bloom, Widow Sarah Beam passed away. The village folk came from miles around to pay their respects. Every bench in the little Church was filled. The Bishop spoke a few words and the choir sang, "The Lord Is My Shepherd." The little Miniature Rocking Horse - all newly finished and painted by brother Jessop was placed a top the casket on a wreath of pine and ribbon. Slowly…from far back in the Chapel a tall, thin boy came forward and faced the congregation. A mop of tangled dark hair fell down over his forehead and tears filled his dark brown eyes. "I ain't much fer words, he began. Fact is… I ain't much good at anythin I ever did. I came to Church mostly to find someone to fun with. Since Maw died…Pa ain't home much. I set up a lot of mischief fer the teachers. No one wanted me around. But, Widow Beam…She <u>always</u> smiled at me and talked to me friendly like…even when she knowed I was a troublemaker. She would say "Do ya need anythin at home I can do fer ya?"

Onest in Church the Teacher read us a story from the Bible, called…THE WIDOW'S MITE". It was all about this woman what gave all she had in the world to the Lord. I thought she must be daft- a doin that- bein selfish like I am. But I think the Widow Beam was a lot like her. She gave all the lovin an smilin and doin good she could do fer everyone. I think she loved me - jist a little bit, and I got to thinkin - If Old Widow Beam could love me - onry as I am…Maybe JESUS could love me too. I got down and I ast Him PLAIN OUT - <u>JESUS do you love such as me?</u> And I felt it in my heart He was a smilin and he said, "YES Tom <u>I DO!</u>"

Stillness settled over the little Chapel. Not a sound was heard in all the congregation as he added - I THINK SISTER BEAM WAS A <u>MIGHTY WIDOW</u> FER THE LORD.